LONESOME BEAR

North-South Books

NEW YORK | LONDON

Lonesome Bear

WRITTEN AND ILLUSTRATED BY

Clay Carmichael

Published in the United States by North-South Books Inc., New York.
Published simultaneously in Great Britain, Canada, Australia, and
New Zealand in 2001 by North-South Books, an imprint of
Nord-Süd Verlag AG, Gossau Zürich, Switzerland.

Library of Congress Cataloging-in-Publication Data is available.
A CIP catalogue record for this book is available from The British Library.

ISBN 1-55858-967-8 (TRADE BINDING)
1 3 5 7 9 TB 10 8 6 4 2
ISBN 1-55858-968-6 (LIBRARY BINDING)
1 3 5 7 9 LB 10 8 6 4 2

For more information about our books, and the authors and artists
who create them, visit our web site: www.northsouth.com

*The art for this book was prepared with
pen-and-ink and watercolor.*

Printed in Belgium

To my students,
with love

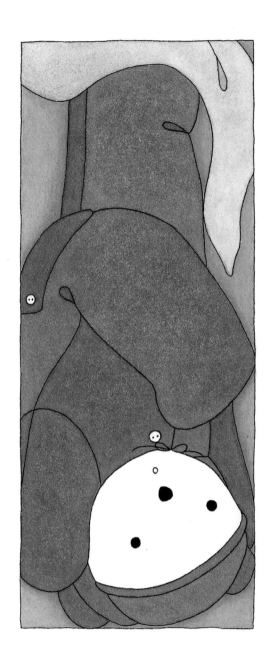

One morning Bear woke up wedged between the wall and the mattress. He had never been wedged this way before.

He often got lost among the covers during the night, or sometimes dreams tumbled him out of bed and rolled him under it without waking him. Always Clara found him.

"Oh, Bear, there you are!" she would say, and take him in her arms.

But not this morning. No Clara found
him or answered when he called. And
when he unwedged himself, no Clara
asked him what he wanted for breakfast

or helped him off with his bear suit.

No Clara was there at all.

Their bed was large and lonesome without her.

He had never lost Clara before.

He looked for her in the bedclothes.

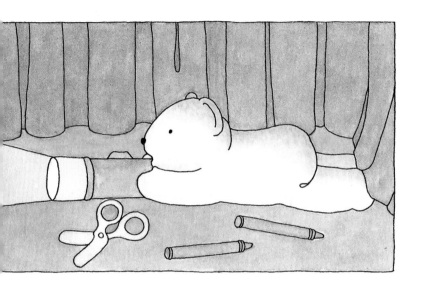

He looked for her under the bed.

He remembered the hide-and-seek
they played on rainy days, and looked

behind the draperies, under the love seat,
and in the toy box.

"Clara!" he called and called, but no one answered him.

He ate a lonely breakfast and wondered what to do.

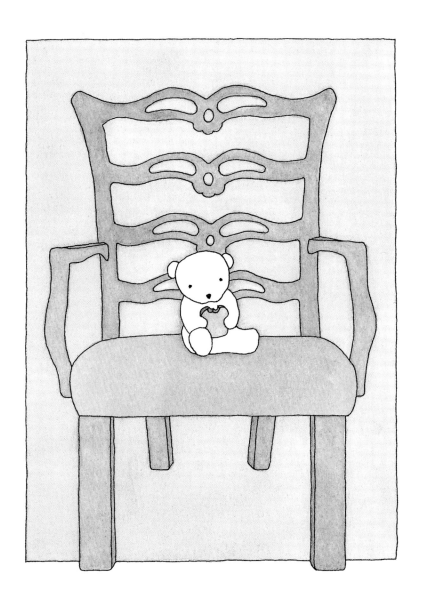

He wandered down to the dock,
feeling very sorry for himself, and
found a little rabbit wringing her paws
and anxiously watching the water.

"They're not coming back," the rabbit said.

"Who's not coming back?" Bear asked her.

"The boy and his family,"
said the rabbit. "We came
to the island last week for a
visit. But as we were hurrying
to catch the ferry, I fell out of the picnic
basket and got left behind.

"I'm a bunny by herself now," she
sighed, and dried a tiny tear.

"I'm a bear by himself," said Bear, and
told her about Clara.

"I'll help you," said the rabbit,
brightening. "We'll make posters and
look for her together."

As they did, they found a stray cat eating melted ice cream and fish heads for breakfast.

"Lost something?" asked the cat.

"Clara," Bear told him. "She was there when I went to bed, but this morning she was gone."

"Why find her?" said the cat. "Now that you're by yourself like I am, you can do whatever you want whenever you want to. You can have ice cream for breakfast if you want."

"But Clara and I eat *cookies* with our ice cream," Bear told him.

"I do miss breakfast in a bowl," the cat said.

"But when you're by yourself, you can stay up all night and sleep all day," said the cat.

"Yes, but Clara reads me stories and keeps me warm at night," Bear said.

"I miss the boy's stories," said the rabbit.

"I do get lonesome now and then," the cat said.

"But when you're by yourself, you don't have to do what people tell you to do," said the cat.

"Yes, but Clara protects me from the big dog who tried to eat me once," Bear said.

"I wouldn't like being eaten," said the rabbit.

"Dogs *are* scary," the cat said.

"Besides, Clara loves me better than anyone," Bear said, "and in just the way I like."

"The boy loved me like that," sighed the rabbit.

"No one loves me at all," the cat said.

But though they looked all day in all the places Bear could think of, they couldn't find Clara.

"I *am* a bear by himself," Bear said. "All alone."

"Like I am," said the rabbit.

"And I am," the cat said.

"Hey, Bear, look at this!" called the cat. "The bear on this poster looks a lot like you."

"So does this bear," said the rabbit.

"And this bear too," they both said.
"You've been looking for each other!"

"Oh, Bear, there you are!" Clara said,
and took him in her arms.

They celebrated with cookies, carrot sticks, and ice cream in big bowls for supper.

And then they made a new poster that said *found*.

About the Author/Illustrator

CLAY CARMICHAEL grew up in Chapel Hill, North Carolina. She studied at Hampshire College and at The University of North Carolina, where she was awarded highest honors for her poetry.

Her first picture book, *Bear at the Beach*, earned a National Parenting Publications Awards gold medal and was published in Dutch and Japanese. Her second book, *Used-Up Bear,* won a *Storytelling World* Award and was published in Dutch, German, Japanese, Spanish, and Korean.

She lives with her mustachioed cat in Carrboro, North Carolina.

*Don't miss
the other books in this series*